Prof. Dr. J. CAL-VIDAL

LEARN TO LEARN

OUR EDUCATIONAL PROCESS
UNDER CHECK

authorHOUSE®

AuthorHouse™
1663 Liberty Drive
Bloomington, IN 47403
www.authorhouse.com
Phone: 1-800-839-8640

First published by AuthorHouse 10/7/2009

ISBN: 978-1-4490-0764-5 (sc)

Printed in the United States of America
Bloomington, Indiana

This book is printed on acid-free paper.

All creatures inhabiting the earth where we live are here to contribute, each in its own peculiar way, to the beauty and prosperity of the world.

Dalai Lama

To my daughters Josy and Christy who continue to learn to learn despite everything—to them, I dedicate this book.

To Eng. Clécia Carneiro for the extraordinary help she offered me while I worked on this manuscript—to her, I offer my recognition and gratitude.

Acknowledgments

This book is the result of ref ections I have had throughout my extensive academic and scientif c career. During my forty years with universities in Brazil and abroad, I have found authentic professors who have shared much more than the typical classroom notions. Some stood up as my role models, and their example is depicted in the pages below.

Many of the concepts presented here arose from conferences I had offered to research students at my university. I extend my gratitude to all who disagreed with me and forced the review of certain concepts and conceptions. Many of these students remain unnamed as they offered their valuable contributions in diverse settings, such as congresses and technical meetings, over the course of my academic life. It was their participation that brought about this book.

This book is dedicated to my graduate students—my best colleagues and friends. With them, I learned to learn and was able to transfer this stimulating experience onto others. I expect that this exercise will continue among the readers of this work.

To educate well does not mean to do everything in the same way. Each individual is not only unique, but he is also a true world unto himself and is able to receive knowledge as long as he has the chance to offer it.

Contents

Preface

In today's world, the challenges in science and technology are growing in all f elds of knowledge and human research across all nations.

The technological evolution in Brazil is very slow and beset with many problems. These problems are often solved through improvisation. Also, Brazilians read very little scientif c literature. Much of what is read and the information that is received comes fragmented through several academic and research avenues.

The excessive emphasis on course work and the sheer volume of information—much of which is obsolete—often compromise the creative potential of our students as they undertake activities other than those that help students gain understanding and experience.

At the undergraduate and graduate levels, we use the classroom extensively; in many cases, the classroom constitutes the main resource of the educational process. Very few courses use the library, as evidenced by beginning research students' diff culty in using this valuable resource.

Worse yet, we don't train young generations how to learn to learn. They are not learning to think. They develop a highly mechanistic and rudimentary mode of processing information, which prevents them from applying logical reasoning in their future areas of study.

We live in a country that has circumvented creativity for a long time. Everything made outside our borders is copied, with little attention to the foreign patent laws. This preference for copying is revealed in the lack of professionals with the ability to innovate their f elds, and this preference f nds its origin in a university that has lost its main objective.

Those who advocate for the massif cation of our higher education are wrong. This highly demagogic process reduces our university education to very dangerous levels. It is necessary to train our students properly as a country needs well-trained professionals capable of solving its social and technological problems. Millions of people with university degrees will never achieve this goal.

Considering studies and simulated problems from the agricultural, industrial, and social spheres, one can obtain aptitude and formation with independent study and consultation with others. Our university students must be connected with, and participate in, full-time research projects and the exchange programs with centers of renowned merit in Brazil and abroad.

In our country, we have professionals who transfer their didactic experience to students through the university. However, there are others who have experience in more modern and effective methods. It is to these latter ones that I turn the hope of our students and research trainees.

1
Our
Educational Process

To begin with, this title is misleading. There is no such thing as an educational process. Process means mass production or production on a large scale, and we do not manufacture anyone. No one is educated on an assembly line. No one is a mass product. The f rst idea that I wish to convey is that the university cannot be a processing plant. We are not all "designed" similarly.

The massif cation of the university

The essential questions are the following: *What brought us here? Why are we born? Where are we headed, and what do we want?* We must ask ourselves these questions to prevent the catastrophes we have witnessed for a long time. A frustrated man or woman is an atomic bomb in motion. Our vocation must precede our formation. The f rst problem found in the Brazilian universities is related to the excessive concern with increasing the number of annual vacancies without relating this purpose to the concept of "where are we headed, and what do we want." I know two very happy people. One of them is a Russian butcher, currently a cab driver in New York. The other one is a Mexican shoe-shiner who works at the international airport of the same city. They are the two happiest human beings I

4

know in the world. They sing, laugh, and are happy while they work because they are doing what they like, and they like what they do. We must f rst discover what we want to be and then achieve the objective God has set out for each of us. We have a mission for our lifetime that each one of us must identify with.

It is impossible to do anything well without enthusiasm. It is the basic ingredient in any research project, shined shoe, or painting f nish. Different investigations and studies have shown people achieve a greater or lesser degree of achievement based on what they desire. The world offers some examples of this reality. It is important to begin something that we are enthused with, whatever it may be, and carry on with it. The individual is measured by his or her results, which are obtained through various factors like strong enthusiasm. Ultimately, effort is much more important than the number of classroom hours spent in a particular school or university. In some cases, university degrees may even become ostentations or labels with little tangible meaning.

There are other ingredients that may favor or limit the realization of what we want most. Many times, fear prevents us from doing what we truly wish to pursue with respect to professional options and different f elds of study. Our society often makes demands for titles that we may not be well suited for, and those with the courage to answer their calling always f nd a friendly hand at the "other end of the bridge." Each one of us must discover our own path and follow it with courage and faith.

For some, marketing themselves is a great drawback. Others don't understand concepts like being or having.

They believe it is necessary to have in order to be and only accept the idea of being before having with diff culty. This notion is casting our young professionals into an abyss where money is the unfortunate criterion for f nding one's calling. Money has nothing to do with success or fulf llment. We must convey the importance of training the mind to think. To think is to transform an observation into something new or different. This does not necessarily mean a metamorphosis; it could be dissecting some known entity to discover another.

The thinker is a creative being par excellence who is capable of solving or developing a problem or theory in an unconventional or unorthodox way. The history of science is full of good examples. As educators and scientists, we must take on the commitment of instilling in our students and associates the capacity to lead through observation, analysis, and imagination. In today's world, I believe that there is a signif cant difference between a thinking person and someone who can hardly see the world around him—a person who only copies and does not create.

The classroom

The apparent pragmatism of the classroom misleads, limits, oppresses, frustrates, and turns people into less than what they should be. Life is a journey—an opportunity to exercise the capacity to think.

Freedom of thinking

Fear and apprehension can compromise our capacity to think in that they interfere with the degree of freedom we need to carry out our thinking activities. The privilege of taking part in university activities must be understood as a unique opportunity to exercise our leadership and thinking in a society that lacks both. I cannot understand an educational system that is not conscious of this role. Most of all, we must be free—

taking this term to its broadest sense, including having enough free time to experience the present moment creatively as much as possible. Our mind cannot be occupied with what is unnecessary.

To think and create is an activity for a select few. Scientif c research is the noblest activity in a university. It is what truly establishes the excellence of a renowned institution. I would say that scientif c activity in our country serves as a true educational mission, which conveys knowledge by teaching through doing as opposed to teaching by listening. The formation of a true leader takes time and demands exercising imagination and action—something diff cult to f nd in a system where passivity reigns.

Scientif c research and education

A good idea can be more worthwhile than all the resources allocated to a university every year. I also would like to emphasize the importance that a good mind can make a difference in a country or the world. A true scientist is not bought with money, and money does not drive his scientif c work and endeavors, either. Unfortunately, we only remember this great distinction when, as scientists and educators, we do not confuse the products generated in our laboratories (e.g., powered fruits, etc.) with the real products (i.e., thinking beings).

Products generated in a laboratory

Our students need to have greater contact with the world they eventually will confront. An agronomy student, for example, must familiarize himself with what happens on a farm or something similar throughout his university studies. He must become involved in problems outside of the classroom. Full-time research projects must be part of the curricula of scientif c-technological courses.

Learning by doing

Our professors participate in advanced training programs in the country and abroad, generating a critical mass of great scientif c merit as evidenced by graduate activities, a key factor for the improvement of professionals entering the system. But the effort to improve our human resources does not seem to have any effect on traditional undergraduate programs, which still use outdated educational methods. The transfer of experiences gained by colleagues trained abroad must be more emphasized than the traditional classroom

A leader or thinker can only be considered as such when he has a good command of himself. It is this self-control that permits us to have a stronger grasp over our surroundings. To love someone, I need to love myself f rst. If we were able to discover the potential on what we most desire, we would be able to develop a force of inf nite reach—a power capable of moving mountains.

A good command of oneself

The creative process, as we have already mentioned, includes observation and the ability to think, including the ability to transfer information and ideas into images that constitute imagination—literally, a particular image put into action. An idea without action lacks results or meaning. Curiosity is essential in life and a *sine qua non* to be creative as researchers, professors, or educators. Curiosity channeled toward analysis and discovery is essential in order to understand the behavior of nature. It is this reality where the endless source of knowledge f ourishes. Trees, f owers, and leaves are all very rich in details and colors. Right now, in areas around my university, a true festival can be seen with the change of leaves. As we see the phenomena closer, it is possible to fnd answers to complex problems in such a richness of detail that it is more visible than what we f nd in the laboratory. The creative process has an extraordinary ally in nature. Great scientif c discoveries are based on the analogy it offers continuously. Curiosity is not a privilege; it is something anyone can acquire.

We all have obstacles to overcome (e.g., language, basic science, etc.); we have to overcome these diff culties within the context of f nding ourselves. It is possible to remain paralyzed for any reason. If we are sincere and want to win, all obstacles are surmountable— even in education. I feel that the universities of Brazil receive extraordinary support in a variety of ways and from a variety of sources despite the problem of massive education programs, which I condemn. At this time, our laboratory receives support from federal and state agencies, which greatly elevates our work and effort. Imagination is very important, but hard work is necessary to get results. We can dream, but we also must perform. We must insist, create, err, and repeat. To begin again and again....

Faith, work, and support: constant needs

To obtain results, we must accept sacrif ces. Several years without supportive resources may be necessary until we achieve an acceptable record. Self-respect is also necessary to carry out projects and achieve goals. Personal growth is the result of a continuous, systematic effort to reach near perfection. Such exercise helps us to be and do better. We simply cannot stop. We must not get off the train of life unless we do not want to embark on our journey. If we are sure of what we want, we must continuously insist on pursuing it.

Finally, we continue to suffer from a grave phenomenon I identify as chronic mediocrity, which is responsible

Chronic mediocrity

for the low incidence of creativity observed in our universities. Such a situation promotes the excessive practice of copying as manifested in multiple ways. Mediocrity can have its origin in a physical-organic def ciency or in an environmental conditioning process that lacks stimuli—perhaps as a consequence of an oppressive school system with little creative tradition. Mediocrity has a decisive inf uence on the press, politics, and even the university, where its pseudo-leadership can produce damaging ferments. Mediocrity is a cancer which must be recognized in many places.

Excellence and merit

We can always improve. We can be better every day if we are willing to be so and to try. We must pursue excellence in our work and in all endeavors. Excellence is not something that labels a particular institution with a title of renowned merit. It represents a comprehensive effort we all must make every day in the frontier where we f nd ourselves. We must vehemently pursue the example of existing systems and model institutions in countries of renowned scientif c and technological advances.

2
The Era of
the Copybook

It is almost nine o'clock in the morning. While I walk through the few green areas of my university, I f nd some students sitting on the grass, all with thick copybooks under their arms. Some are discussing parts of its contents somewhat nervously. Another "partial test" is about to take place, and the copybook is the only resource they have to complete another stage of their careers.

What is most alarming is that the copybook is a main component in their educational process. Someone once told me that it goes from student to professor without major alterations, and the implications of this process are truly compromising.

What I observe at the university is repeated at the lower educational levels. I can take my two daughters as examples. They spend every morning writing in a copybook what their teachers write on a blackboard—boring and outdated information. She transfers to the blackboard a tangle of news, whose main purpose is to be passed to a student's notebook. The student transfers this information only because she is concerned about what will be on the partial test. In this scenario, little emphasis is placed on the library, the true repository of books, which has fallen out of use. As such, it is in need of renovation.

In this system, what is learned most is how to copy and memorize. I would say that, in our country, we copy everything because it is precisely what we learn in our schools at every level. Besides its stifling oppression, this process limits creativity in its broadest sense. The excessive passivity during exposition and copying in our classrooms leads to the inability to learn how to learn, to learn how to observe, and to learn how to think.

Copy and memorization

I clearly observe this situation with my graduate students in my laboratory. Most of these students had never had the opportunity to consult a classic technical book, don't know fundamental components of nature seen under a microscope, and are unable to draw conclusions from observations of the most fundamental physical phenomena.

The act of thinking is demonstrated by the capacity of drawing conclusions from very simple observations. Throughout the years, individuals have made great discoveries through *accidents* because those individuals have been prepared to make that discovery. It is impossible to discover anything if we do not learn early how to observe natural or induced phenomena.

Learning to think

During a recent stay in Canada, my two daughters, ages twelve and eight, went to a little school in Vancouver. When I visited their school, I was truly amazed. The classroom was a zoo, with countless pets of all kinds. The children were kept occupied observing behaviors, reactions, and other phenomena they gathered from the pets.

The Canadian educational system

Another group had magnifying glasses and other resources. They wandered through a little forest to discover spiders, toads, and everything else imaginable. They were learning how to observe; and on more than one occasion, I saw them running to an impeccable library where they found more details about what they had discovered in their forest. It was a true process of learning how to learn.

The issue that I raise is far from amusing. Unfortunately, we are experiencing a tragedy in terms of education in Brazil and some other countries. The classroom is an abominable process that only makes sense if it is intelligently complemented with a good library, the undertaking of long or short internships, the participation in full-time research projects, the mandatory exposition of our teachers (at any level) in order to induce more eff cient educational systems as in countries where there is real evolution of the educational process (e.g., Germany, England, Canada, and the United States).

The classroom in Brazil

I recently read in a book about the importance of action as it relates to information. I would say that aptitude and formation are what we truly need to offer to our youth. By aptitude and formation, we understand the development of a capacity before what is new. Besides the ability of learning to think, it is a very important to be able to innovate and create. Our country must possess one of the briefest histories of invention in the different technical-scientif c f elds. Certainly, this dearth relates to our most tradition of copying!

Copy in excess: a dangerous reality

One of the most unfortunate causes of this situation resides in the problem of not learning to think. This inability naturally leads to mediocrity in the individual. This mediocre fellow can be anywhere—in the schools, in the universities, in the press, in politics, in the government. An individual who fails to learn to think in due time reaches adulthood without the minimal faculties necessary to make original and intelligent decisions. He simply does what he can without being able to establish clear leadership. He usually repeats what he hears, is inf uenced by rumor or the news, and performs in his studies or his occupation well below average.

A country with a high rate of mediocrity, aggravated by an uncontrolled growing population, is taking giant leaps toward the precipice. We have to stop the mediocre and demagogic vision that defends mass production within our universities. We must revise educational concepts at all levels. We need to eliminate this miserable blackboard and notebook. They gradually destroy the inventive capability of our young generations, giving birth to adults who engage in mediocre thought.

The blackboard and the copybook

Our country urgently needs leaders and thinkers!

3
The Crime of "Editing" Study Notes

I do not know exactly how this practice began. The fact is that "editing" study notes was established in our country with the same force as the copybook and the blackboard. Overnight, everyone began to "produce" notes. Someone had good study notes of the "subject" from the previous year and decided to publish them, although in the most rudimentary way possible. Over time, the process was perfected. The teachers themselves became the authors of a publication that began to receive different names, even in disciplines in which they had not made any contribution.

Even ignoring intellectual rights of authors, this type of clandestine "publication" commits a greater crime: it distances the students from good reference books. With this instrument—each time more incomplete and more condensed than the previous version—students substitute the habit of reading renowned authors of telegraphic works with imperfections expressed poorly and, at times, in ambiguous terms.

Study notes and their defects

The industry of study notes grew over time. It began with the famous preparatory courses for university entrance exams and later reached the secondary school and universities. In secondary schools, they were so shameless as to be able to establish agreements with

The complicity of educational centers

educational centers to establish the obligatory purchase of their notes with the school tuition.

The process is absurd in several ways. First, it universalizes the use of a study source that lacks any technical-scientif c value, seriously compromising the education and preparation of our students. Second, it distances our youth from contact with good books and classic reference works, which puts the quality of our university students and professionals at a serious disadvantage as compared to academics from other countries. Third, it creates in our students the habit of doing everything in the shortest and easiest way possible. Notes are an easily digestible substance, which prevent the use of broader and more concrete analysis and reasoning. And f nally, the concepts of *learning to learn, learning to study,* and *learning to think* are seriously compromised in a system that relies almost exclusively on notes.

Several days ago, I made a dramatic experiment in my own home. I had refused to pay part of my daughters' school tuition as it included study notes. One of my daughters is taking science and was already strongly accustomed to the use of study notes. When I interrupted the "supplement," she was furious and turned my home into a true war zone.

When things calmed down, I patiently gave her some classic books of chemistry, physics, analytical geometry, and other subjects from my private library. I explained the advantage of studying from them for their richness, detail, and clear exposition. I left these classics on the table and left the room. Shortly afterward, I saw the books piled on a shelf where we usually keep old magazines and things of little interest.

The books stayed there a few days until I decided to take them back to my library. My daughter had decided not to consult their contents at all. Books were truly something strange to her, and she never even considered delving into them. My daughter was addicted to notes to such an extent that she is now totally at the mercy of this easy path. The word *addicted* is absolutely the right word, and I have a great task to get her back to using original sources.

What happens in secondary school is repeated in higher learning. What is most tragic is to recognize the fact that even among those professors trained abroad, the addiction to study notes can occur. When these colleagues were studying in the United States or in England, they must never have studied from notes. Still, the long use of this fateful instrument in our country has led some of them to join the club, putting at risk not only the degree of excellence of our educational programs, but above all the basic competence of our young professionals.

I know some colleagues and educational authorities reluctant to accept my positions, which some consider radical. The issue is not so unlike the process that adult birds use with their chicks while they are in the nest: unable to f y or to swallow the food commonly found by the adults, the parents break down their food and then give it to them until the young birds learn to survive independently. However, in our educational reality, the baby bird never leaves the nest; it never learns to f y; and the adults continue to offer it everything in well-broken-down chunks in the notes and on the blackboards of our secondary and higher education centers.

There may be others who ask how can something so damaging and destructive endure unaffected throughout the years. Study notes do have a way to *facilitate* everyone's job. After having made the notes, the teacher satisf es the will of the great majority of his students who prefer to have the subjects clearly def ned on the partial test. Likewise, with the notes, students *presume* to have isolated what is "most important" and will not need to "lose time" studying relatively unfamiliar books. The program coordinators do not take this into account. Their main preoccupation is to increase class hours, regardless of how those hours are spent. Truthfully, this increase in hours in our secondary or graduate courses is also an "invention" of ours. With the lack of good preparatory programs, a considerable volume of superf cial information was "invented" to be presented to our students. The universities in Brazil have the illusion that, by tackling as much information as possible, they will reach perfection. Most understand their specialty very little and much less in depth. Our undergraduate students only discover this when they enter graduate studies where, despite all the defects, something is achieved in areas most related to research. It is by doing research that our youth are convinced that, by doing and not simply listening, they will learn something truly new.

Advantages of the study notes

Brazil needs a great educational revolution. It will certainly come on the part of responsible colleagues and out of the interest of many young students disillusioned by an inadequate system for their academic training and real professional competence.

4
The Mission of the University

The Formation of a Leader

Contrary to what many people think, it is not possible to form leaders with the exclusive effort of the university. The *formation* of a leader presupposes the convergence of personal characteristics in a given individual. A series of **Institution leader** outcomes, wills, and determination can eventually lead to a leader's emergence at a certain moment of a person's life. Leading university institutions in different f elds of study and research have a high probability of creating leaders who were not their graduates. Scientists from all over may experience a discovery in a given moment of their scientif c development, promoting themselves to leadership roles. The Nobel Prize, for example, distinguishes scientists as pioneers with recognized merit. To be a leader means to arrive f rst in the f eld of study—showing the way and having the opportunity to participate in an advanced study with unique possibilities to contribute to the f eld of knowledge and discovery. Leading universities that I **Being f rst** know—like Harvard University and the Massachusetts Institute of Technology (MIT) in the United States— have many Nobel Prize recipients among their teaching and research faculty. These universities have several characteristics in common, the most evident of which is their extraordinary capacity to identify and develop advanced, unprecedented studies. To be f rst, we must not fear the unknown. To open paths presupposes a disposition and will to know what is new and unexplored. In the case of a scientif c institution which has the ambition of becoming a leader, it must make sure that it has a constant f ow of scientists with the possibility of leading and proposing projects in such advanced levels that will allow the host institution to become a leader in some f eld of research.

The Ability to Think

To think does not mean to meditate about something preestablished, nor does it mean to be amazed by something surprising or to contemplate the planetary system vaguely and constantly. To think presupposes a capacity to observe, followed by the possibility of forming images to reach unprecedented conclusions. It was this ability that turned Madame Curie and Fleming into pioneers. To observe is more than just looking. It is to imagine what is beyond the observed painting. Thus, with observation comes imagination as result of thinking and creativity. There are those who learn how to observe and to imagine, and they are creative beings. The world needs this type of human being very much to f nd imaginative and creative solutions for so many of the problems we face. The world needs thinkers. We have more than enough people who copy and repeat. We are tired of redesigning models developed abroad. Countries like our own are in urgent need of people to end hunger, to defend green spaces, to combat the pollution and poverty that surround us, and to stand up to the barbaric system that enters our homes daily and unexpectedly destroys the very imagination of our children. The world is tired of this. But where are the leaders to stand up to this state of affairs? There are scientif c leaders capable of stopping the process of

Creative being

Leaders needed

degradation in the world we live in. I insist that the world needs them to help us f nd new solutions.

Our True Destiny

We all have opportunities. All of us. We just have to learn how to choose the correct path from our very early life. If we want to be idiots our entire lives, we will so be. We only have to follow everyone and experience the consequences. To be a follower is what we will be if we do not learn how to f nd our own paths. The world is full of the fearful, of people unable to be and to think. To evaluate what we most want is a way to begin to believe in our own destiny. It is always feasible to f nd a world of possibilities in our lives if we accept the signs that God offers us. We will f nd our true destiny from the moment in which the will to serve is stronger than that of being served. Beyond that, it is necessary to develop the idea of being and to understand that having is a consequence. The world needs people who are. For example, a country like Brazil urgently needs people who can lead our agriculture scientif cally and technically. The possibilities of service exist and are endless. If you want to be truly happy, think about the idea of serving. And from this, you can live without boundaries.

Leaders without boundaries

The World Has No Borders

We all have the right to live a dignif ed life. God did not build it in vain. And I am not going to repeat the Gospel here, but I can guarantee you that God extends his hand to those who have the courage to begin a life of service. Many times, we do not perceive Him at our side as clearly as when we discover Him in distant lands—far from the comfort that annihilates us. You must cross the bridge or take a plane. He will always be on the other side. Think about the possibility to grow. With your characteristics, you can go far and will not be left at the wayside. Armed with your training, you can be useful in some countries where the existence of people with your qualif cations is extremely rare.

At certain times, we feel a horrendous fear that translates into a lack of faith to confront an unknown reality. We all prefer to experience what is familiar to us and, in this way, avoid the challenges that can help us to grow. To know ourselves, we must leave the common environment we live in. There are people who can testify to the favorable results that an environmental change has made in their lives, in the yearning to obtain better professional training in the true spirit of service. A considerable number of professionals who worked with me can attest to this fact. Most did not know what they would f nd when their undergraduate studies ended. The majority did not return to their homes because they were chosen to take important positions in other parts of the country. And they all discovered that they were more capable than what they had imagined.

Faith and spirit of service

Growing and Offering

But none of this would be possible if the longing to grow did not exist. Whoever does not want to grow accepts the minimum that he is offered and, thus, spends the rest of his life accepting less than what he is capable of. In order to grow, it is necessary to want to grow. I cannot grow if I do not wish to do so. I grow when I serve. The main objective of my work is to make sure that some of those who cross my path change their attitudes and conceptions. This will certainly be my legacy: to change some lives for the better. The day that many colleagues understand the reach of this mission, the world will be better and our own existence will make more sense.

Knowledge, Action, and Imagination

The difference only becomes apparent when we are before a challenging situation. Many things that had f rst seemed impossible become possible. When we confront a challenge, we think we cannot surmount it, **Limit of possibility** technically or personally. The limits of what is possible are determined by the capacity for action and by the circumstances that can be imposed upon the situation. Einstein said that knowledge was not as important as action. The many notebooks with all the theories accumulated throughout one's years of schooling mean very little. None of this means anything if we do not take action. And it is unfortunate that so many have diff culty understanding what action is. I know of cases in which individuals changed the course of their lives when they went on international trips, and the simple will and capacity for action changed their lives completely.

According to what we have previously expressed, imagination results from the process of observation. It constitutes the great difference between a creative individual and one who is not. Knowledge is not as important if we lack imagination. Every institution and every individual need imaginative capacity to stand out in a highly competitive world. Scientif c creation, for example, cannot dispense imagination since knowledge is a support of minor importance in this context.

Exercise Your Thinking

When we exercise our thinking, our vision broadens. Our mind can be stimulated daily to confront new challenges, or we can simply promote its stagnation. A good way to achieve this is to sit in front of any newspaper or television channel in our country. This practice will lead to incredible toxicity, a highly lethal dose for the future. We need to learn how to exercise intellectual activity intelligently and constructively. All great discoveries and all solutions to problems facing us today will come about from the capacity to think and the vision of a few prepared for it. The mediocre will stay behind, sitting in their chairs, watching their videos with images from their past. Participation without the effort that thinking requires will never be possible. It is the men and women of vision who have learned—many times in distant lands—that practices and endeavors yet to come may make a difference.

The intellective activity

Essence and Thinking

To do something repeatedly means to think repeatedly because almost all of what we do we think about in some way. If you go to a bar every day to cause an uproar, you will become a specialist in uproars. You will enter the next bar, and you will be a doctor in this subject. And you will possibly do only this. The library is right in front of you, and you never visit it. You only go there if you have an obligation to read material from the library, and you eventually attend a seminar there if it offers an attractive certif cate. Then this is what you are—it is what you do repeatedly. I think that many of you are a little lost in our university because you make bad use of your time. The excessive programming in the classroom makes it more diff cult to use the library

The bad use of time

more intensively, to carry out small research projects in your areas of interest, and to participate in curricular internships during the course and a series of activities that would improve your knowledge.

To Believe in Circumstances

Before the most diverse circumstances that we confront in our lives, we have to believe. It can be good to change a little. Why don't I go do that internship that they offered me in Rondônia? "I heard there is a commission there to protect the trees that are threatened by f re, and they need volunteers; they only offer lodging. I took notice of the ad but put it aside." This could be, who knows, an excellent opportunity to have a better vision of reality. In the best-case scenario, we must believe in the circumstances. Who knows if we will f nd the path that we are looking for at a given occasion?

Human Will

In everything that I have said up to now, there is a little determination and human will. And this is an individual project. I cannot follow the exact path my colleagues follow. The ideas that each one of you has about an academic and professional future are not the same as those of colleagues sitting next to you. It is not possible to copy each other because the world needs us as individuals. We can eventually develop future projects that coincide or relate to one another's, but they will not exactly be the same ones. The plans of life that await us are not the same; they are unique. Therefore, we must understand that these programs do not accept the idea of collectivism. The duplication of decisions is a fatal error many commit, tearing their own professional futures apart. Before deciding on a

A different path for every one

future based on that of others, it is necessary to listen to yourself and understand the signs. These signs are diverse and arise from various sources.

Much of what we say is the result of an experience. It is diff cult to talk about anything that we do not know. This testimony is the result of a tested process that I hope can help some to f nd their own destiny.

Enthusiasm and Triumph

We come to this world to be happy. We come to conquer. To reach our true destiny and collaborate in the Divine Work that is unf nished. And we must labor on this Work. We are not a totally completed divine work. A way to perfect ourselves is to collaborate as enthusiastically as possible on this Work. There are many things that the ambitious do to destroy everything.

The Divine Work

Experience is always the sum total of what is done. What have you done? Have you only listened? It is necessary to act as well. If you want to acquire experience, you must do. In fact, you only learn by doing. By listening, you learn almost nothing. It is from what you do that you will be able to learn.

What Is Training?

The term training is applied erroneously to many pseudo-academic and pseudo-scientif c activities. The model we have in Brazil insists on making graduate research programs include disciplines from different areas. In many cases, I do not consider graduate programs advanced training when they compromise the development of the main activity itself—to do a project. It is from this development that advanced training really arises.

The development of a good mind allows paths to open. A good mind will certainly open new paths for your country and for many things that you cannot imagine. Put your mind in charge. If a scientist, educator, or professor does not have a good mind, he will be unable to control his own destiny or that of those who go through his training program.

Developing a good mind

Power and Action

The idea of power is narrowly linked to the idea of action. Everything that has been put forward here attempts to clear up concepts so that we can become better human beings. I believe that we all have a chance. What we need is to become better on an ongoing basis, using the great resources that we have at our disposal. I hope that somehow I have helped someone follow the path that God has reserved for him. I hope that all of you can learn to be truly happy.

For a better human being

5
Research: Learning by Doing

To kill a simple mosquito will only be successful if you concentrate. Dispersion does not construct anything; therefore, learn how to concentrate. The study environment differs little from a true sacred temple. The same atmosphere of embracing and ref ection is necessary for a person who prays or learns.

Preliminary notions

Our Portuguese language is imprecise in many ways. Many terms used in science and technology are imprecise, as opposed to their counterparts in English. The term *pesquisa*, for example, means little to many people. Its equivalent in English, *research*, gives an idea of searching again and again. In this way, to investigate does not only mean "searching," as many think, but searching many times. Research can only be done by those who are willing to search, repeat, reencounter, reconsolidate, reach, and re-search. And research is learning by doing.

And what is learning? In English, this process precedes *knowledge*, which means the know-how acquired through the most diverse means or systems that can take us to what we generally call "learning." *To know* presupposes the command of a particular area of knowledge, which can only be reached through the appropriate means and mechanisms. The simple idea

What is learning?

of learning by "watching" is like participating in a theatrical play without having the opportunity to place ourselves in the reality created by the play or scene. I question any educational means in which educating is merely a passive agent that cannot intervene in the process of obtaining knowledge in any way. This does not differ substantially from what we understand as information, whose reach has the limitation of news and whose "shelf life" is always very short.

Be very careful! A person can have much information and not know anything! I can be an individual who reads many books and still be a complete idiot. As opposed to knowledge, information does not assure us the command or capacity to solve problems in the world we live in. Information without knowledge means nothing. It is a painting on the wall that calls our attention but contains no message whatsoever. It is an abstract "work."

The concept of doing is not linked to the concept of time because "time" is not a trustworthy parameter. Time is a witness in a situation or condition of a given experiment. The term "effect of time" does not make sense, because such an effect does not actually exist. There is the effect of physical parameters— like temperature, relative humidity, or speed, whose attributes can be measured over a certain period of time. In this case, what happens with natural phenomena is applied to the greater phenomena. However, as opposed to many natural phenomena whose processes are governed by very precise and simple laws, man has a high degree of dispersion and is able to carry out his tasks over different times through extraordinarily complex factors and means.

"The time effect"

In this way, similar activities are carried out by people in different times.

The notion of time and the notion of doing vary considerably from person to person, depending on habits, traditions, self-discipline, mental attitude, etc. Thus, what corresponds to a minute to one person can become an hour to another. Consequently, some do and many simply pseudo-exist. The process of learning by doing presupposes behavior of scientif c rigor, which cannot omit either the eff cient use of time or the correct choice of what to do. The latter will constitute a separate subject that I cannot consider at this time.

To Observe: Preliminary Notions

A thinker could never exist if there were not an observer. It is impossible to think without observing. Many people believe that "thinking" corresponds to a more or less ordered process about something whose expression does not yet possess a clear "def nition." In the majority of cases, thinking results from a capacity that we can all develop through the exercise of observation and interpretation. What is normally known as imagination is, in, reality the capacity to transfer real images into a given perspective capable of generating "new knowledge." Many discoveries have been the result of this process. Some of the most celebrated scientists of humankind have used this simple skill to carry out those advances that have benef ted so many of us. There are very impressive examples in Newton, Fleming, Curie, Einstein, and others.

To observe and to imagine

What does it mean to observe? To observe is not only to look. To observe means to have the capacity of using senses properly and completely. There are many who are unable to stop for a minute and observe a tree, a leaf, a f ower, the richness of a stone, the richness that nature offers us constantly and prodigiously. The number of details that we have before us constitutes a fantastic exercise of observation that many times goes unnoticed. The latest model of a headlight on an automobile f lls our curiosity repetitively and idiotically. Naturally, when I speak of the richness that nature offers us, I do not exclude human beings who can be appreciated more than just for their appearances.

The concept of observation is broad and encompasses much more than the f ve senses. The capacity of perception is the capacity that the mind has to identify and distinguish new situations. This ability can be developed with continuous exercise.

I had an experience in Canada that truly impressed me. I watched eight-year-old children developing observational skills with little animals kept in their "classrooms." The animals were there simply so that the children could study their behavior. The children also made constant visits to the library. It was an excellent exercise in learning by doing and observing. In some recognizably advanced countries, the traditional classroom is substituted for exercises in observation and interpretation of the kind that already exists in the Canadian primary schools. The classroom is condemnable because, in it, we are mere spectators— like birds waiting for half-digested food without leaving the nest. This nest-feeding continues into adulthood, and in this way we never learn to f y. Take the term to f y as learning to use the library, to observe, and to reach

The Canadian experience

conclusions freely and independently. All courses that keep the classroom as the only means of experience are obsolete because they do not allow the exercise of creativity—a primordial function in lower or higher education.

We do have good models that constitute an excellent source of inspiration, which are much richer than our classrooms. Let's take the example of Norman Borlaug, Nobel Peace Prize recipient in 1970. Mr. Borlaug was a fantastic man who left an American university to do experiments in one of the poorest states in Mexico, Sonora. There he developed the Green Revolution with genetic experiments that some know very well. Borlaug is a good example of a man who conducted research in a hostile environment and overcame the challenge because he made use of all his creativity.

Nature is certainly our best school for science. Understand that the simple observation of nature does not allow us to understand it completely. What I would like to emphasize is that the nature surrounding us provides us with the motivation to f nd what we need for the interpretation or experimentation of natural phenomena in good books or the laboratory.

Natural phenomena

Reading and Understanding Science

To read and understand science is necessary to overcome limitations. The scientif c message must be understood in a totally different way from a romance. Reading and understanding science can present us with a great diff culty, especially those who are unmotivated or unable to identify a given problem or study. When we read a romance novel by Simmel, a famous Austrian writer, we can become so fascinated that we end up

The scientif c message

32

reading the whole book in a short period of time. In this type of reading, our imagination travels and manages to participate in entirely new and surprising episodes. To read a scientif c article is a totally different experience. In it, we must be selective, capable of discerning what truly interests us for a given project or study. We must read a message about which we have little initial understanding, especially if we lacked previous experience with or observations of the issue in the laboratory. Reading science implies, above all, the incessant search for answers to well-formulated questions in our mind after having conducted some type of experiment with a given observable phenomenon. As opposed to the romance novel, you should only read scientif c literature if you are strongly motivated.

The educational function of the technical literature

People develop scientif c interests for many different reasons. Unfortunately, in our schools and even in the university, the work to create greater scientif c motivation in our young people is largely limited. Consequently, there is much improvisation at the moment in which one decides to begin a scientif c career with a minimum amount of information and experience.

Scientif c interest in the university environment

The process that we use to obtain what we want is truly simple and encompasses, in most cases, early experiences that mark inclinations that are only consolidated years later. Such experiences are generally associated with a series of values and aspirations that we develop in maturity. The choice will become easier when there is minimal intervention from others— from the family circle for instance—who can interfere in the decision-making process. For example, there are people who are interested in veterinary medicine for

Doing and learning

Choosing a profession

a number of reasons. I hope that the "novelty" and "popularity" of the course are not among them.

In our laboratory, I get graduates in engineering who wish to work on projects that my group offers them: retention of aroma in dehydration processes, induction of crystallization in lyophilized fruit sugars, cryopreservation of frozen fruits, and microstructure and architecture of food systems. These research lines constitute, above all, an opportunity to study phenomena with the application of principles of food engineering. The challenge involved in problem solving, which always come up in the development of the resulting projects and sub-projects, constitutes the possibility to learn by doing. Here we are not concerned with the direct production of dehydrated or frozen fruits. What we strive for is the ability of the human mind to generate knowledge through observation and to develop the capacity of synthesis by reading objectively and understanding science through the development of the notion of learning by exposing oneself to the environment of the scientf c reality.

If someone prefers to be a musician or f lm director on the other hand, please do not pay any attention to me. Go forward in search of your ideal and be what you truly want to be. You must be what you most desire independent from all the advantages and disadvantages considered by others. Do not be tempted by vices of any kind like "f eld of work," "salary level," "status," and so forth. We should place ourselves at the service of a superior destiny, capable of turning ourselves into the architects of a Work that never ends. It is much more important "to be" than it is to have! The world needs people who are true to themselves.

Be happy. Be what you want most!

What Is Doing Science?

Doing science does not involve a simple training exercise. It does not mean to try to have command over a particular area of knowledge, which is consolidated into a certain volume of information. It cannot be understood as a way for promotion to obtain degrees or something similar. Doing science is the best way to reveal the secrets of a particular part of nature in a given f eld of study.

By doing science, we become involved in the inf nite possibilities to exercise and broaden our power of observation, which, as we have already emphasized, is a fundamental condition to develop the action of thinking in a true and complete human being.

Nature gives us inf nite possibilities to study and discover. Within the most diverse f elds of human knowledge, the possibility to experiment still exists. The available material resources do not matter so much. Whoever does science can establish professional bonds and relationships with any research center all over the world and participate in opportunities for personal integration in multiple national and international scientif c meetings and events.

A true scientist can make an enormous difference across the world at a time when we need urgent solutions for hunger, the destruction of our green resources, overpopulation, poverty, increasing crime, incurable diseases, climate changes, and so on. The world needs a few excellent scientists, men and women willing to give of themselves before thinking of themselves in each new era.

We are in need of good scientists!

What Does Learning Mean?

Contrary to what many may think, learning does not mean the accumulation of large amounts of information to appear more illustrious. I can be an illustrious man and be unable to confront any new situation that might arise during a normal day. This can happen in my personal or professional life.

Some think that learning implies reading everything that we get our hands on, to guarantee the realization or "command" of a certain reality. This process is somewhat similar to what we observe in a "sponge." With the same ease with which we absorb something that seems "new" to us, we stop retaining that information after a brief lapse because it lacks importance to us over time. To learn a particular technique or experience in order to guarantee employment can be interesting at f rst glance, but this strategy becomes meaningless when we discover that we must be something more than mere instruments of an incomplete society when it is viewed exclusively from the perspective of functional productivity and *performance*.

What learning is not

To learn means to acquire an instrument capable of arming us with skills to confront what is new within the f eld of study or of work in which we are acting. To learn, we must always be linked to the idea of growth and the ability or disposition to offer something to the f eld. Only people who acquire a f exible mental structure can learn and be capable of responding quickly and eff ciently to unusual situations in their f eld of action.

Learning and what it implies

Information and Formation

What is the true mission of the university? What does it mean to form people?

Certainly, we cannot "form" anyone by exclusively offering him information. Formation without the acquisition of ability makes no sense whatsoever. In real life, to possess knowledge, purely and simply, means very little. In many situations, we need to know what to do. A doctor can know everything about human anatomy and be unable to diagnose an illness because he does not know how to act before a particular case.

A mechanic who has taken many courses about modern automobile technology might be unable to discover a particular defect in his own automobile. **Formation and** Formation means having the capacity for imagination **action** and action. Even the most inventive can attain few results without the necessary action to consolidate a particular idea or venture. The world is full of dreamers who achieve little or nothing because they did not acquire the necessary capacity to materialize what they desire. In one's personal and professional life, it is the results obtained that truly count.

I cannot understand formation without truly developing the capacity to think. Any educative process that does not search for this objective does not deserve to be **Creativity: its basis** called educational. Because to innovate or create, which presupposes the discovery of something new, we must learn how to observe and think—minimal conditions for the creative process, which is the principal reason for an educational system that aims to form individuals with the conditions to confront a reality that is constantly changing and transforming. We must produce an original individual with the ability to confront what is new with a few instruments in order that he understand and resolve each situation as something natural in his life within his chosen f eld of work..

Some Interesting Advice

Read less, and do more.

Limit your area of interest to a minimum scope.

Do not think about how much you should earn but in what you can honestly offer.

Do not take a course (or something similar) because someone makes you.

Know yourself completely, and be your main adviser.

Learn how to observe and reach conclusions independently and objectively.

Make use of experimentation as a way to know the truth.

Do not defend or aff rm concepts about which you have no command or solid experimental basis.

6
Vocation, Performance, and Credibility... and What about Creativity?

These concepts have very different connotations from what they really are. The f rst three can converge into what is known as creativity, which, in the f nal analysis, is what makes a difference in a given individual, institution, or country.

What Is a Vocation?

A vocation is not something that comes from others. A vocation is not the result of group thinking. I must not study engineering because my class has decided to do so. In fact, a vocation is a call to serve. All of us receive a call that can come in a variety of ways, but it usually arrives in a unique and special manner that, at times, is diff cult to believe and accept; and for this reason we fail. A vocation is the beginning of a path that must be taken very carefully. Whoever errs in his vocation or calling makes a mistake forever, promotes an imperfect marriage that will be diff cult to break up afterward. I know that I am exaggerating a little here, but the truth is that taking the wrong path from the start will make a person unhappy his entire life. A vocation is not something for us, but for others. A professional life only makes sense if it is designed to

A call to serve

serve, to offer something important or necessary in the country and world we live in.

What Does Performance Really Mean?

This term is somewhat confusing for some. It is taken from engineering and means the capacity of a particular machine to produce or carry out preestablished operations for certain periods of time. For us, it means the *performance* of a particular person to undertake the most diverse of tasks, the majority of which are outside his area of action or competency. Performance can be something false that does not convey the real merit of a given individual.

What Purpose Does Credibility Have?

Throughout our lives, we receive credit under different circumstances. Our families, at times, offer us hope, which can be translated into limitless credibility. As we grow, we receive the credibility from institutions, which also expect some type of "return" from us. When we reach adulthood, society and the world demand attitudes and contributions worthy of our position and responsibilities. This type of credibility is actually a projection from others, which does not correspond to—and consequently, contributes very little to—the professional competency expected from each of us. Credibility can be given to a particular university, which naturally cannot be evaluated by the grandeur of its physical structure but rather by the real contributions from its professors and researchers in their areas of inf uence.

University credibility

Creativity and Its Crucial Role in Innovation

Creativity entails the capacity to integrate all available resources to produce something new. It means little to "produce" many scientif c papers to guarantee a desirable credibility. Scientif c and technological advances depend mainly on innovation, and high-level scientif c research must make maximum use of creativity to promote the f ow of resources for its maintenance and implementation. When we refer to creativity, we refer to good minds. They are part of a process that germinates from a given idea or observation and takes shape in the imagination of truly privileged individuals capable of transforming something ephemeral into an indisputable reality. Knowledge does not always constitute the great difference, but the vision we have of a given problem. Some of these are still crucial in virtue of the somewhat unscientif c treatment they receive. Such is the case of hunger and the continuing destruction of nature.

Brains and creativity

Hunger and the destruction of nature

Our Scientif c Reality

The problem with the lack of creativity in some regions of the world is aggravated by the exodus of minds to countries that offer greater stimuli. In Brazil, this loss is signif cant each year. The United Nations ranks the top one hundred countries in an index called "Human Development," which takes into account educational levels, health, social well-being, scientif c evolution, environmental protection, among others. In 1998, Brazil was in the seventy-fourth position, which ref ects a dramatic situation for a country like ours. We need to reverse this situation. We need to generate real leaders capable of transforming our current

Human development, Brazil

situation into something more promising in each of the aforementioned sections. In scientif c activity, this leadership must exist with greater authenticity. It makes no sense that at a time when we need to promote leaders in our universities, there are still people who do not support scientif c research, inhibiting the creative potential and evolution of our scientif c status and evolution.

This promotion demands the solid participation of elements in conditions of offering support and approval in a particular scientif c setting. It is teamwork directed at a single objective: to reach the desired result. In our case, the marginalization of scientists who return from abroad with many ideas and projects and with extraordinary possibilities of leadership is common. These scientists should take part in important decisions in different spheres of our educational development. Their marginalization constitutes a serious obstacle for the evolution of our graduate and research programs.

Marginalization of scientists

The culture of our universities must be transformed into something more dynamic in order to achieve signif cant changes overnight, even in our way of thinking. There must be a real shift in our abilities to observe, imagine, and think. This change, if properly integrated, can have an enormous inf uence on our university. This model of effort contradicts the excessive centralization that we observe in our high-level institutions. Despite the merit and productivity of certain individuals, the centralized model, to which we are all subjected, reduces the creative input of scientists signif cantly.

Centralization at universities

How to Improve Our Performance

Since our main activity is scientif c in nature, it is worth emphasizing what true performance means. True performance will only be possible at the moment we manage to reduce performance that is less relevant. Secondary mechanistic activities that demand some degree of concentration and a minimum of creativity can seriously compromise good performance. This will only be possible with exclusive and constant dedication to creative work and a life of excellence over the years. The multiplicity of interests can dissipate energy and concentration while preventing a high level of scientif c action. Science has no frontiers since a work of merit in a particular laboratory can have repercussions in any other country. Performance implies an extraordinary power of selection (in a given scientif c f eld) and daily dedication toward that purpose. A vocation continues to exercise an important role in advanced training, turning young graduate students into professionals with a better chance of achievement.

Performance and selectivity

The Basis of Scienti f c Training

As we previously indicated, people and institutions give us credibility somewhat freely. In the scientif c world, credibility is not achieved so readily. In general, the youngest scientists run into resistance from the more prominent ones. In some cases, the institution itself or geographic center in which a laboratory is localized can contribute to a greater or lesser degree of credibility given the existence or a lack of scientif c tradition. When an individual begins, he has little scientif c credibility even though he may have a certain maturity and disposition to conduct science and research. It is the perfection of these characteristics aligned with a strong work program that will improve his scientifc confdence throughout the years. This effort must include a constant persistence, obedience to high moral patterns, and a continuous state of alert—characteristics of the scientifc truth. This constitutes the self-fulfllment that many must exercise. This process is very slow and can take years for a particular work to receive recognition. In science, the exercise of truth follows the discovery of the phenomena, its principal driving force.

Advanced training in our universities continually runs up against differences between the candidate's background and the level of master and doctorate programs. A great work must be carried out to break with old customs and insert a new mentality. Our results are not tied to the transformation of products with industrial potential but to the conversion of an individual without any scientifc credibility into a being—at least a beginner in his career—who will change his life forever. At frst, any person with a minimum of theoretical fundamentals in disciplines in the scientifc branches and good experimental training in particular felds of study can become a scientist of merit if he knows how to promote continued self-growth through dedication to his feld.

Scientist of merit

Other factors that must be developed include a capacity of superior concentration, audacious and brave leadership, and a perspective that is simultaneously humane and scientifc. With these characteristics, it is possible to earn international credibility. This is related to several facets in the world of science. For many, it is a closed club with few possibilities of access. But above all, science demands a dose of professional maturity. Maturity generates greater mental ordering,

44

allowing an extraordinary increase in the capacity to perform and create.

The Price of Success

To succeed in life or in any scientifc career, it is necessary to concentrate all resources and efforts in a given direction. This concentration demands many sacrifces. Throughout our journey, we may be tempted many times to accept positions and assignments that, by their very nature, do not correspond to our scientifc inquiry. Science loses a signifcant number of members each day who are won over by private initiatives, public service, administrative positions, and other activities moved by vanity, money, and the lack of motivation. The price of success is the award that arises—in the most diverse moments—from a work crowned with international recognition and with the respect of those in an infnitely broad and rich club. It is common to f nd a new collaborator in some congress that we might attend in Toronto or Budapest or to meet people who truly wish to participate in our effort in a given research project after knowing our studies. In this context, our geographic location matters very little, but the contribution we are offering to the world does. What matters is our creative and productive capacity to solve or place into perspective the solution of problems with social, economic, educational, or technical transcendence. It can also be pointed out that the expressive majority of the candidates that we receive for advanced training end up offering important scientifc contributions to our country and the world and, therefore, occupy important academic and scientifc positions. This is also the price of success!

International recognition

In Search of Scientif c Merit

Doing science demands a constant perfection. This only becomes possible with continued self-discipline, faith in the work, and creative capacity. Much of the time is spent on what is invisible, on something that exists but cannot be easily perceived. The true scientist must transfer this same discipline, the same faith to the young people he is transforming. Without discipline, there will be no results; and without results, faith loses its reach. Another very commonly discussed issue in the scientif c community is related to the ambition of the researcher. There are many who are content with little—those who think that a discovery could not be possible in their laboratories. Others, however, have greater expectations and, even in their smaller numbers, tend to be responsible for great advances in science in the past and in the present.

Research and ambition

There are many who work on, more or less, "compact" modes, interrupting their "turn" during conventional periods. This functional reality corrodes self-discipline and fatally leads to mediocre scientif c production, affecting the merit of the researcher and his institution. Scientif c activity is a thinking activity par excellence, where each members must exercise this condition in daily unconventional moments. The ideal is to work as continuously as possible, no matter where and when the scientif c activity can be exercised and the thinking permitted. A painter and many other professionals work with their hands. A scientist is a thinking being and must be understood as such. This does not exclude him from being human, experiencing the problems of a highly disordered and undisciplined world. But yet, he must demand of himself a dedication to science within a convulsive, imperfect world. A rigorous

Organization and self-discipline

organization and discipline are necessary to carry out a daily schedule of scientific commitments, which are simultaneously common and uncommon.

In a country like ours, recognition moves very slowly, and many times it never arrives to professionals who deserve it. For some, merit is a rarity because, when not recognized, they feel that they lack something out of their reach. In science, it is important to have merit and be recognized for a given contribution or discovery. The problem of evaluation and recognition, however, resides in the difficulty to identify components of merit capable of translating the innovation or discovery—considering its economic, social, educational, or environmental impact—into a promising reality. Abroad, notably in the most advanced countries, recognition is practiced whenever a given university or research center develops contributions with a certain degree of projected merit. In places where merit goes unrecognized, the exodus of minds takes place to the detriment of production and creativity. In certain cases, an exaggerated incentive to promote individuals with an essentially administrative or mechanistic activity becomes transparent.

Merit and recognition

University Promotion in the Scientific Setting

Independence and collaboration in research are not bought; they are won. Contrary to what the royalty assures to their descendents, I cannot enjoy any scientific recognition without having demonstrated competency and credibility. Freedom and other values that permeate the academic world are repeated every day in our laboratories, which receive associates uniquely and exclusively on the basis of merit and background. I cannot accept anyone by favor or promote someone who does not have the abovementioned requirements. Sometimes, we can be confronted with tragicomic situations that result from differences of individuals' personalities, which expose themselves to big challenges. It is common to confuse sympathy with scientif c skills. Mutual collaboration is only possible with personal aff nities, strong technical capability, and great harmony in the f eld of work.

The Universality of Scienti f c Activity

Scientif c activity is universal. You can work with Greeks, Muslims, Jews, or Anglicans. We have already had in our research group Americans, Russians, Poles, and Indians. At this time, we have illustrious representatives from Latin America (i.e., Peru, Bolivia), and we are building relations with colleagues from such diverse countries as New Zealand and Canada. A few years ago at an international congress in Toronto, I saw a poster of a Polish colleague who caught my attention about the excellence of his results of his scientif c inquiry. Soon, this colleague was located and immediately invited to work at Lavras. I believe that this is an excellent example of collaboration following the patterns stated in the previous section. Scientif c activity offers the possibility for strong human relationships above any condition of nationality, belief, regimen, or party aff liation.

Scientif c activity and human relations

Beyond this, there are many possibilities of representation at different levels in society, a condition that can offer additional opportunities of participation and contribution. History has registered several condemnable episodes with scientists: the use of nuclear f ssion for destructive means, the use of chemical weapons, germ warfare, and defoliant agents—which represent a great threat in our time. But the condition of a scientist presupposes an individual with the constant mission of being a problem solver and pacifer, which grants him free transit in areas of confict in almost all parts of the civilized world to resolve today's problems.

The Power of Criticism

Criticism is necessary in science and in the academic world. It is impossible to make substantial changes in the world in which we live without a good dose of criticism. Specifcally, the evolution of science experiences the power of criticism to fnd its own direction. Some societies reject criticism for fear of fnding the truth. Some people fear criticism because they are insecure and consider it a threat to their false convictions. We must all accept criticism to reach the near perfection that we pursue in our work. I would say that, without criticism, we remain stagnant at the levels in which many countries whose scientifc activity is very poor. What is at play is the opinion about the issue itself. The author, institutional origin, and secondary relationships matter very little in science. Criticism is necessary mainly when you have the authority to do it. You can preserve or promote the good reputation of the person responsible for the contribution while the object itself is vetted or criticized.

True Human Development

True human development is the result of a number of factors. Every individual who is part of a given research group at a given university must generously exercise the recognition of merit, the power of criticism, the constructive praise, and the authority of a scientif c leader. Science is a dignif ed and honorable vocation where the individual practices mutual respect, compliance with the greater and lesser laws, and—above all—the rare capacity to understand the true reasons of workings with nature. True human development, to my understanding, will only be reached on the day when all human beings—scientists and non-scientists alike—respect with the same dignity and honor all that God has created and know that we do not completely understand everything. Development does not mean having more and more, but being more each day.

7
Mediocrity: Our Greatest Threat

I am now in the waiting room of the dean's off ce of an important Brazilian university. On a center table and on the couches are all kinds of publications, bulletins, and newspapers with different formats and printed in a variety of sizes. The impression one gets is that people in this country cannot do anything very well. Even at the level of our universities, the display I have before me indicates that almost everything is mediocre. The contents and design are of very bad taste.

Brazil is taking a giant leap toward an abyss. If I examine the newspapers displayed in any kiosk or if I stop in front of any television channel, the answer is almost always the same: our country is submerged in a climate of foolishness and stupidity.

Whoever selects our news or produces our TV programs is certainly convinced that the audience thinks at a very low level and that the only way to guarantee a larger audience is to offer something as mediocre as possible. What is worse is that these professionals are right. Each year, we have many people who enter adulthood, the job market, politics, and different professions who demonstrate very low intellectual achievement and professional qualif cations.

The problem is alarming and can only be perceived by a few. It is almost always noted by those who have been away from the country for some time and had the possibility to live with people abroad.

One of the f rst things that can be observed is that the majority of people here have not developed their capacity to think very well. Many decisions are improvised at numerous levels.

Improvising law

With great ease, people return to the copy method, to the generalized opinion, to the superf cial solution—to what is cheap and easy.

To our understanding, we pay a high price for having allowed prohibitive population growth in this country. Too many people are born in too short a time, and the majority grow up and become adults in hostile conditions.

Most of our citizens come from large families; many lack the minimum conditions to place a complete, physically and mentally speaking human being in the world. Many Brazilian children are born and survive to face nutritional, psychological, educational, environmental, and other obstacles. Our systems for housing, public education, and health services are unable to attend to an ever-increasing demand.

Population growth

In a poor country, such as ours, these consequences are truly alarming. The balance between existing resources in the nation and the population pressure is becoming more lopsided every day.

People who grow up in adverse and, sometimes, infrahuman conditions become underequipped adults.

Roots for incompetence

Their *performance* remains well below the norm, but they still enter the productive systems of public and private life while performing poorly. This results in the proliferation of incompetent professionals in numerous sectors of our society.

A country without good minds cannot prosper. Children in excessive numbers—malnourished and lacking in other respects—will never reach adulthood with the minimal intellectual capacity to become thinking beings worthy of actively participating in the social and constructive life of the country.

I am surprised to discover that our authorities in positions of solving our grave population problem still have the illusion or the false belief in thinking that a populous nation is a necessary condition to becoming a powerful nation. Those who believe that we must f ll our empty spaces with new compatriots are only fooling themselves. In fact, the empty spaces of today will matter very little to a population that is overcrowding our major cities and generating the social, environmental, and security problems that we all know very well.

Population vs. powerful nation

To be strong and dynamic, a country needs quality people from their heads to their feet—not just their feet. It needs a few well-constituted, well-trained, and well-intentioned people capable of offering before thinking about problems or receiving benef ts. The country needs people with a spirit of service, people unafraid to change what is wrong, people who do not conform so easily.

Having many people in a poor country is, to a certain extent, a luxury that we can no longer afford. I believe that all of the ministries and authorities who can give an immediate solution to this problem must put all of the resources to work to end this true national disaster.

Brazil urgently needs to save itself from this grave threat—that of becoming a mediocre country for not having controlled its population growth.

Control of population growth

Index

Printed in the United States
by Baker & Taylor Publisher Services